Tell Me Why

a girl god book

Written by Trista Hendren

Illustrated by Elisabeth Slettnes

www.thegirlgod.com

Other Girl God Books for Children

The Girl God
A book for children young and old, celebrating the Divine Female by Trista Hendren. Magically illustrated by Elisabeth Slettnes, with quotes from various faith traditions and feminist thinkers.

Mother Earth
A loving tribute to Mother Earth and a call to action for children, their parents and grandparents. Writen by Trista Hendren and illustrated by Elisabeth Slettnes.

The Animals Know It
A book designed to remind children of their empowered state of being. Complete with wisdom from the animals, bright, colourful images to trigger the imagination and colouring sheets—this book will entertain and delight. Written and illustrated by Arna Baartz.

My Name is Medusa
The story of the greatly misunderstood Goddess, including why she likes snakes. *My Name is Medusa* explores the "scary" dark side, the potency of nature and the importance of dreams. Arna Baartz gorgeously illustrates this tale by Glenys Livingstone, teaching children (big and small) that our power often lies in what we have been taught to fear and revile.

My Name is Inanna
Tamara Albanna weaves the tale of Inanna's despair, strength and triumph—giving children of all ages hope that the dark times in life will pass. Arna Baartz illustrates this journey with beautiful paintings of the owls, lions, stars, sun and moon that direct Her. *My Name is Inanna* is dedicated to Tamara's beloved homeland, Iraq—The Cradle of Civilization; the Land of the Goddess.

My Name is Lilith
Whether you are familiar with the legend of Lilith or hearing it for the first time, you will be carried away by this lavishly illustrated tale of the world's first woman. This creative retelling of Lilith's role in humanity's origins will empower girls and boys to seek relationships based on equality rather than hierarchy.

My Name is Isis
In this fresh look at the ancient Egyptian Goddess, Susan Morgaine reclaims Isis as The Great Mother Goddess and The Giver of Life, from whom all things come. Arna Baartz mystically illustrates Her as healer and protectress. *My Name is Isis* is a treasure box for children of all ages who want to draw close to this wise and nurturing Mother Goddess.

My Name is The Morrigan
The Morrigan remains one of the most misunderstood goddesses of the Celtic pantheon. Her mythology is a tangled web of various guises, deeds, and battles—and even her name is a bit of a mystery! Dive into the world of the Goddess of Death, and learn about what The Morrigan really has to teach us—and, maybe you'll find that She, and death, aren't so scary after all!

www.thegirlgod.com

For boys, young and old... but mostly for Joey.

His blue eyes sparkle like the stars
His love is like the sun
My boy is my heart and my soul.
The day you were born my heart sang—
and, the world stopped—at least for me.
E-v-e-r-y-t-h-i-n-g was different.
My Joey, you are the son, the moon, the stars,
the joy, the love, the oath, the hope, the dream
and the everything that I always wanted
and always knew would someday come.

On a dark day, sometime near the end of the world, a mother sat on a
bench with her only son to ponder what would become of humanity.
Not knowing how many days she had left, the mother turned to him and
blurted, "Let me tell you something, Joey."

"It is only when we truly know and understand that we have a limited time on Earth
and that we have no way of knowing when our time is up that we will begin
to live each day to the fullest, as if it were the only one we had."
-Elisabeth Kubler-Ross

The day you were born was a hard one for me.
A month early, you were anxious to see the world- to be out of
your solitary confinement and get on with your life. You were so
quick, there was no time to prepare. Three pushes and you were
out the door! Looking back now, it seems your short life has gone
by just as fast. I was mostly on my own and sometimes it was all I
could do just to get our basic needs met.

"The two most important days in your life are the day you are born, and the
day you find out why." -Mark Twain

I wonder if I have taught you all the things you need to know to live well in this cruel world. I question if you know just how much I love you. I look at your long, stretched out body and I want to put you back with me. But I can't. So here are all the things I would say to you if I could rewind. (Just in case I forgot some stuff.)
You were wanted. You are worthy.
You are a child of God/dess.

"I love and accept you exactly as you are." -Louise Hay

When in doubt, be kind.
Be nice to your sister. Be nice to all girls!

My creed is Love;
Wherever its caravan turns along the way,
That is my belief, My faith.

-Ibn al-Arabī

Reflect on the wisdom of your Grandmother.

"In the quiet stillness of your heart
you can hear your Grandmother's voice.
Listen.
Her wisdom shines in the Light of the stars."

-Grace Alvarez Sesma

Don't spend time worrying. Things always seem to work out, eventually. The Universe will support you.

"To the mind that is still, the whole universe surrenders." -Lao Tzu

Read voraciously.

"You must write, and read, as if your life depended on it." -Adrienne Rich

Give and accept as many hugs as possible.

"We need 4 hugs a day for survival.
We need 8 hugs a day for maintenance.
We need 12 hugs a day for growth."

-Virginia Satir

Laugh. Watch funny movies. Spend time with people and animals who make you happy.

"Happiness is a spiritual value." -Z. Budapest

Take long walks—or whatever you can do to clear your head.

"You have learnt so much, and read a thousand books.
Have you ever read your Self?
You have gone to mosque and temple.
Have you ever visited your soul?"

-Hazrat Baba Bulle Shah

Climb and plant as many trees as you can.

"Trees are great teachers. The trees are great listeners.
That is why we should meditate in their presence.
The Great Spirit is in every rock, every animal, every human being and in every tree.
The Great Spirit has been in some trees for hundreds of years.
Therefore, the trees have witnessed and heard much.
The trees are the Elders of the Elders.
Their spirits are strong and very healing."

-Mary Hayes

Don't waste anything.

"If not for reverence, if not for wonder, if not for love, why have we come here?" -Raffi

"Mom, I know all that!" Joey said exasperated. "Tell me a story. Tell me why the world is the way it is."

"Who told you the stories that taught what it meant to be human, and did they have your best interests at heart?" -Mark Gonzales

His mom thought for a moment and then began to share this tale....

"In a time of destruction, create something." -Maxine Hong Kingston

There once was a boy who loved a girl. They played together all day. They climbed trees, built forts out of blackberry bushes and formed mud patties. They played hard until night fell and they needed food and rest.

"Those who contemplate the beauty of the earth find reserves of strength that will endure as long as life lasts. There is something infinitely healing in the repeated refrains of nature—the assurance that dawn comes after night, and spring after winter." -Rachel Carson

They did everything together. They were partners and cohorts. There was never an unmet need for either of them because they shared what they had and worked together when food was scarce.

"It is love, not philosophy that is the true explanation of this world." -Oscar Wilde

The boy loved the girl as much as he loved himself.
And she loved him back with all her heart.

Let your love flow outward through the universe,
To its height, its depth, its broad extent,
A limitless love, without hatred or enmity.
Then, as you stand or walk, sit or lie down,
As long as you are awake,
Strive for this with a one-pointed mind;
Your life will bring heaven to earth.

-Buddhist saying

One day, they ventured out a little further than usual. The boy saw a gorgeous piece of fruit that he instantly desired. It was different than anything either of them had ever seen before. The lusciousness of the fruit made them realize they were really hungry. The girl knew that they shouldn't take something that did not belong to them, but the boy had to have it.

"It takes a great deal of courage and independence to decide to design your own image instead of the one that society rewards, but it gets easier as you go along."
-Germaine Greer

Despite her efforts to dissuade him, the boy climbed over a fence, jumped into someone else's yard, and reached for it. Scared for her friend, the girl followed him.

"Never ever again will I accept that someone else's reality is mine, just to make them happy."
-Kristen Johnston

Once he saw the beautiful fruit, he took it. Just as he was about
to bite into it, he saw the girl peering at him with annoyance.
He held it out to her – "Here, you take the first bite."
Pleased with his generosity, the girl bit into the fruit.

"Remember that not getting what you want is sometimes a wonderful stroke of luck." -The Dalai Lama

Out of nowhere, a large old man appeared. He was angry. "How dare you steal my fruit!" He grabbed the girl and shook her really hard, knocking the fruit out of her hands. The boy was scared. Instead of taking responsibility for what he had done, he agreed with the old man.

"Truth is the only safe ground to stand on." -Elizabeth Cady Stanton

She was a *bad* girl. It was he who had tried to convince her not to take the fruit, but she hadn't listened. He changed the story to make himself look good.

"I've learned that people will forget what you said, people will forget what you did, but people will never forget how you made them feel." -Maya Angelou

The girl was a loyal friend. Even though she couldn't believe what was coming out of the boys' mouth, she didn't have the heart to contradict it. She said nothing. The old man patted the boy on the back and thanked him for trying to save his fruit. He gave him a piece of his own to eat while he scowled at the girl for her crime.

The boy savored the sweet fruit. It was the most delicious thing he had ever tasted. Although it pained him to see the look of betrayal and hunger in the girl's eyes as juice dripped through his fingers, it tasted *really* good. Could he actually eat the entire thing, in front of her, and not share it? Before he knew it, the fruit was gone. The girl looked away, wiping the tears from her cheek.

"There is a proverb that says, 'Talk so that I may know who you are.' But I say, 'Show me your eyes and I will know who you are." -Nawal Al Saadawi

"Come on home!" he commanded her. She lagged behind him, no longer an equal—or a friend.

"Love is or it ain't. Thin love ain't love at all." -Toni Morrison

As time went on, both the boy and the girl began to believe that she was somehow inferior. They lost their closeness. His needs became more important than hers.

She became a diminished version of herself.

"No person is your friend who demands your silence, or denies your right to grow." -Alice Walker

He found the girl less and less interesting. She wasn't fun to be with anymore. She didn't want to get dirty. Her appearance became more important to her than what she could accomplish. She started to be dependent on him for what she needed instead of getting it herself.

"Listen—are you breathing just a little, and calling it a life?" -Mary Oliver

He started to re-write the first stories they had been told, reversing the order. Instead of the world coming to existence from The Great Mother, it was Father God who had birthed them. This made no sense to the girl at first, but over time, she accepted it as fact, correcting her other sisters when they dared bring up The Great Mother.

"Men, too, need the feminine divine in order to reconcile with, recover, and honor the repressed and denied feminine aspects of their own being and becoming." -Jane Caputi

He began to hoard more and more, sharing less with her. She
started to slave after him, picking up his messes and cooking all
his meals. He went out alone and played with other boys
instead of her. He began to make fun of her for being a girl.
"She wasn't nearly as strong or as good at sports," he told her.

"Words have the power to shoot down or raise up. Sharp cutting words can whirl for years."
-Louise M. Wisechild

He and the other boys began to compete. Everything became a clash for more. But the more the boy acquired, the less happy he felt. While he ate the best steaks, the girl ate a small bowl of porridge and was often hungry. While he shopped extensively for himself, the girl wore the same dress over and over.

"Money heals nothing, though it can take the edge off pain.
Only one thing in all the world has the power to heal: love."

-Malika Oufir

The boy was lonely. He remembered how much fun he used to
have with the girl, but his pride wouldn't let him apologize.
He was sure she would hate him.

"My grandfather used to tell me that life was a dream.
He also said that when people finally realized this,
the dream could be changed, and then humanity would change."

-Don Miguel Ruiz

One day, the boy grew tired of what his life had become and wondered off in frustration. He fell into a giant hole deep in the ground. He slid further and further down until he was squatting in the darkness, gasping at all the dust he'd inhaled.

He tried to scratch his way out, but it seemed futile.

He called for help, but no one could hear him.

"There is a life-force within your soul, seek that life." -Rumi

The girl was frantic looking for her friend. She searched everywhere. When she finally found him, she was scared. How could she possibly get him out of the hole? She was too weak; too fragile. She couldn't possibly lift him out by herself. All his new friends were out hunting for more stuff. There was no one who would come soon enough to help him. He was doomed.

"When we do the best we can,
we never know what miracle is wrought in our life,
or in the life of another."

-Helen Keller

They both began to cry from the depths of their hearts. Feeling as though his life was over, the boy gave up his pride and apologized for everything he had done. "I'm sorry. I'm just so sorry. If I could get out, I would make everything right again," the boy sobbed.

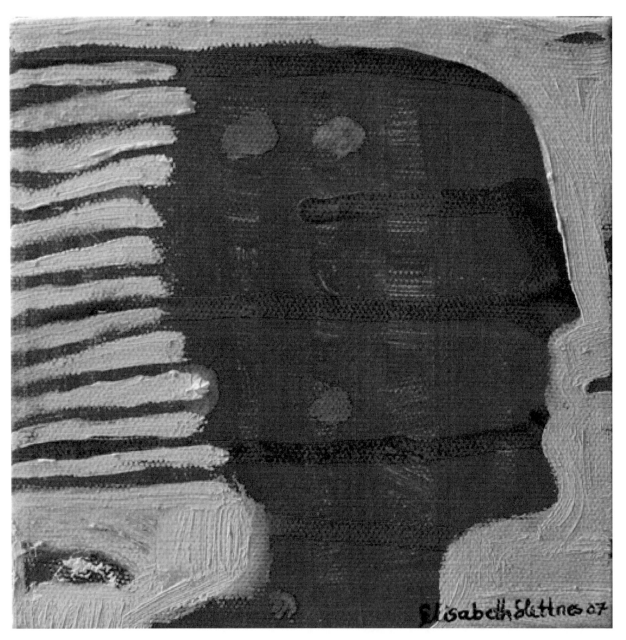

"Proper apologies" have three parts:

What I did was wrong.
I feel badly that I hurt you.
How do I make you feel better?"

-Randy Pausch, *The last Lecture*

Hearing their cries, other boys and girls began to gather around and listen. They realized that they were all in the same boat and needed to act quickly. One by one, they joined hands, and shared their strength to pull the boy out of the hole.

"Action is the antidote to despair." -Joan Baez

They vowed from then on to always work together. The boy shared everything he had with the girl and treated her as he would like to be treated. And they returned to being best of friends.

"Our feelings are our most genuine paths to knowledge." -Audre Lorde

Joey sat up and looked at his mother. He noticed she was crying quietly. He realized it was her story she had told him. And he vowed to help make it right.

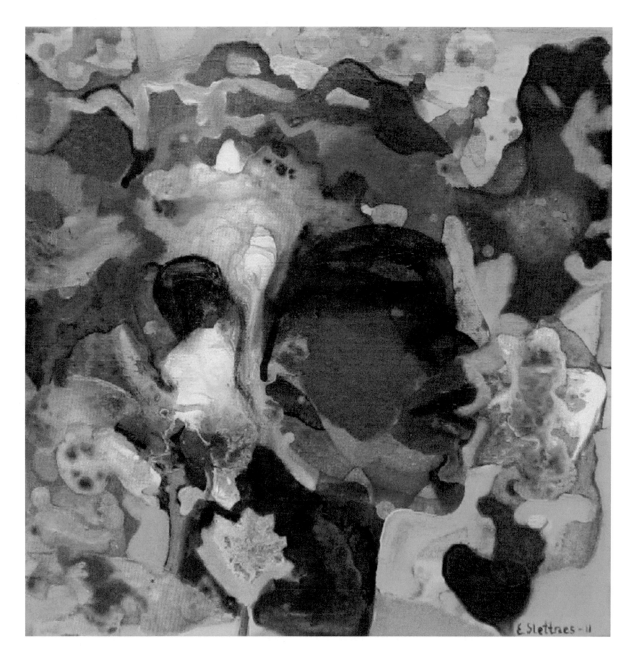

"The time has come to reweave the future with different threads." -Yaakov Jerome Garb

He spent the rest of his life working together (not against) his sisters around the world. Compassion, sharing and love were the foundation of all they did.

"You are the sculptor of your own reality. Don't hand your tools to anyone else." -Jeff Brown

And while they had up days and down days, overall they all lived extraordinarily happily ever after!

"I believe that imagination is stronger than knowledge.
That myth is more potent than history.
That dreams are more powerful than facts.
That hope always triumphs over experience.
That laughter is the only cure for grief.
And I believe that love is stronger than death."

-Robert Fulghum

Trista's Acknowledgements:

Joey: You have given me so many laughs and so much love. You are the sweetest boy I could ever have asked for. Your intellect amazes me constantly. I love you in a way I could never imagine and probably never will adequately express. "You will move mountains kid."

Love and light to my stepchildren, **Ferdinand** and **Carl-Richard**: May you become kind and loving men like your father.

Love and blessings to my first nephew: **Jesse**.

Special thanks to my beloved husband, **Anders**, for his tremendous contributions that made this book possible.

Many thanks to my mother, **Pat**, for help with editing, babysitting, and everything else.

Many thanks to my circle of closest friends: Alyscia Cunningham, Liz Hall Magill, Bridget Robertson, Desiree Jordan and the many beloved women who have supported and encouraged my work. I love and appreciate all of you.

Lastly, it has been an honor to work with **Elisabeth** and **Morten** again. There's no end to how much I admire Elisabeth's talent and how grateful I am to both of them for their contributions to this book.

Elisabeth's Acknowledgements:

To **Trista**, kindred spirit and inspiration, for her wonderful drive and vision, patience, and faith; for her love and devotion to my art and for choosing me to participate in her magnificent and important book.

To **Morten**, my beloved husband, handyman, driver and computer wizard. You are my source of inspiration, advice and love, for all the work and time put into the book, and in my artistic work in general.

To **Anders, Pat**, and all the skillful and dedicated helpers out who saw the importance of this book. Thank you all so very much.

To my friends and family, for believing in me and backing me up to believe in myself as an artist.

Kristin and **Marianne**, for being best friends as well as sisters and faithful audience at most of my exhibits.

My mother, **Ingeborg**, who has passed along her warmth, care, and universal love. Always by my side.

My father, **Olav**, who introduced me to drawing and visual art, saw the talent in me, backed me up in choosing the path of arts, and encouraged me to learn more and seek knowledge.

Last but not least, to **Joey,** and all children, for asking those wonderful questions that make us look deeper into existence.

Quotations

Whenever possible, we obtained the blessing of the author. Below, you can also find the websites of authors quoted in the book, if available. It is with gratitude and appreciation of these beautiful words that we quote them in *Tell Me Why.*

Elisabeth Kubler-Ross - ekrfoundation.org

Louise Hay - louisehay.com

Grace Alvarez Sesma - curanderismo.org

Z. Budapest - zbudapest.com

Raffi - childhonouring.org
From the song, Tomorrow's Children
(Inspired by Riane Eisler)
Words & music by Raffi
© 2002 Homeland Publishing

Mark Gonzales - wagebeauty.com

Kristen Johnston - gutsthebook.com

The Dalai Lama - dalailama.com

Maya Angelou - mayaangelou.com

Sandra Cisneros - sandracisneros.com

Nawal El Saadawi - facebook.com/nawalalsaadawiofficial

Toni Morrison - tonimorrisonsociety.org

Alice Walker - alicewalkersgarden.com

Mary Oliver - maryoliver.beacon.org

Louise M. Wisechild – louisewisechild.com

Don Miguel Ruiz - miguelruiz.com

Joan Baez - joanbaez.com

Jeff Brown - soulshaping.com

Robert Fulghum - robertleefulghum.com

Praise for The Girl God / Mother Earth / Tell Me Why

"The Girl God: a picture book to show girls that god can be a girl, god is inside, god is an idea, a positive action or good deed, god is open to creative interpretation and should be about everyone. A great book to dispel the myth that god is male with wonderful illustrations by Elisabeth Slettnes. Empowerment for our girl children." –A Girls Guide to Taking Over the World

"This is a delightfully rich book that can spark conversation and reflection on many levels – and one worth returning to again and again." –David Weiss, Author of *When God Was a Little Girl*

"This book is a must for our daughters." –Christy Turlington

"*Mother Earth* is a book for the ages, one that parents should read to their children for generations—for its message of healing is one we must take to heart." –Elizabeth Hall Magill, Author of *Defining Sexism*

"The story form of the message of environmental awareness brings it home in a personal way. The illustrations by Elisabeth Slettnes are a big part of the appeal, as are the quotations. I highly recommend *Mother Earth*." –Marilyn McFarlane, Author of *Sacred Stories: Wisdom from World Religions* and *Sacred Myths: Stories of World Religions*

"Trista and Elisabeth have created another gorgeous illustrated story to impart wise, holistic values...this time about our environment, and done elegantly in metaphor and narrative. If only every child received this book from her or his mother or father, how differently we might treat Mother Earth—with gratitude, respect and awe." –Amy Logan, Author of *The Seven Perfumes of Sacrifice*

"*Tell Me Why* uses a reimagined version of the Genesis story of Adam and Eve as an opening to begin discussing the loss of Mother God with children, especially with boys. The book does a beautiful job of describing the loss that boys feel when they are denied the companionship of the feminine side of God and, consequently, a healthy relationship with women in their lives. It is not a book that bashes men or masculinity; instead, it exposes the wounds caused by gender stereotyping and patriarchal religion, while leaving readers full of hope for reclaiming an Edenesque harmony between men and women. This is an ideal companion to the earlier books in this series, *The Girl God* and *Mother Earth*." –Monette Chilson, Author of *Sophia Rising*

"Another gem from Trista Hendren and Elisabeth Slettnes. A beautiful and important message to all children, told here in the re-telling and re-writing of the Creation story, to Joey, by his mother. With Slettnes' stunning artwork and inspirational quotes from other writers, it takes its place alongside *The Girl God* and *Mother Earth* as a future classic." –Ruth Calder Murphy, Author of *Spirit Song* and *Dance of the Days*

"Trista Hendren has done it again. Incorporating beautiful pictures, meaningful quotes, and a story line that resonates she has created a wonderful book that will, hopefully, inspire hugely needed conversations between every boy, girl, man, and woman throughout the world." –Peter Wilkes, Author of *A Woman Called God*

If you enjoyed this book, please consider writing a brief review on Amazon and Goodreads.

Made in the USA
San Bernardino, CA
03 March 2019